Tim Wells is made of r
mash, and Leyton Orient FC.

Moonstomp

MOONSTOMP

Tim Wells

unbound

This edition first published in 2019

Unbound
6th Floor Mutual House, 70 Conduit Street,
London W1S 2GF
www.unbound.com
All rights reserved

© Tim Wells, 2019

This book is a work of fiction and, except in the case of
historical fact, any resemblance to actual persons, living or
dead, is purely coincidental.

ISBN (eBook): 978-1-78965-046-4
ISBN (Paperback): 978-1-78965-045-7

Cover design by Mecob

Printed and bound in Great Britain by Clays Ltd, Elcograf
S.p.A.

For Carmilla Karnstein

Super Patrons

Johnny Alucard
Mike Baker AKA King Patty
Paul Barrett
Michael Baxter
Sharmilla Beezmohun
Miki Berenyi
Richard Boon
Janine Booth
Kit Caless
Alison Charles
Sadeka E. Choudhuri
Tom Claydon
Glenn Cooper
Stanley Corona
Mark Coverdale
David Dangerfield
Rob & Sophie Dangerfield
Gwilym Davies
John Eden
Roxanne Escobales
Jonathan Eyre
Jessica Fenn-Samuelsen
Steve Finan
Michelle Fisher
Ged Forrest

Martin Fuller
Don Gosh
Paul Hallam
Chip Hamer
Mark Harris
Brian Harrison
Simon Hughes
Richard Huw Morgan
Marika Josef
Ravi Juneja
Phill Jupitus
Jan Kelly
Dan Kieran
Sarah Kobrinsky
Dominic Lipson Powell
Theresa Macaulay
Bernard Mahon
Gita Malhotra
John Mann
Shiona McArthur
Donna McKean
Ben Metcalf
Dusty Miller
John Mitchinson
Matthew Morris
Stefan Muff
Jan Noble
Katie O'Loughlin
Tim Paine
Sophie Parkin

Nina Penlington
Eddie Piller
Justin Pollard
Suzy Prince
Imogen Robertson
Anne Rouse
Eli S-Deutsch
Sarah Sanders
Scott Seath
Sipreano
Joe Skade
Squire
The Betsey Trotwood
Tim Turnbull
Colin Udall
Julie Vee
Robert Wells
Sarah Wells
Sean Whelan
Matthew Worley
Ottilie Wright

CHAPTER 1

'I want all you skinheads to get up on your feet. Put your braces together and your boots on your feet and give me some of that oooooold moonstomping...' the record kicked in. Sprocket stuck through the hole of the rotating yellow Treasure Isle label, the disc spun on Joe's Dansette. It was 1979 but this record from ten years earlier was still getting people grooving. Reflected onto the deep black of the vinyl, up on its left-hand side, was the moon as it shone its light through the bedroom window.

It was Friday night and Joe Bovshover was back from work with a buff paypacket full of wages. He'd wolfed down the shepherd's pie at the caff, had a behind-the-ears and under-the-balls bath, and was heading out: brogues shined, knife-edge crease to the Sta-Prest, braces over a Brutus button-down, and wedge in his bin. 'Andsome. His best skinhead shmatta. The gear was crisp, smart and an alternative to the trends haute couture was selling. There was a sophistication to Joe's look, as there was to thousands of other kids, be they skinheads, punks, rastas. The sophistication and fine detail was a point of pride, a finely pointed weapon against subservience. He was a full-of-life seventeen-year-old and looking to gain a lot more experience before Monday rolled around again. Sociologists write reams about the alienation of capitalism. We know, we read it. We see ourselves described in those blue Pelican sociology books but never understood. We know all about alienation and capital, we don't need it explained by soft-handed wankers that can't see what we value. We produce style, dance steps, grace. The strange beauty of the murmuration of starlings across the sky, the swagger of mobs through the city.

It was gigs of a weekend; a couple of pints, a smile from a sort, and music, didn't always matter what, but loud music. Music that'd make you pound away the workaday week on the dance floor. It was better than the telly. His dad reckoned the breweries paid the BBC and ITV to screen crap of a weekend to make sure the pubs were overflowing.

Walking down the steps of the Hope and Anchor was like leaving the nine-to-five self behind. The Mithraeum over in Walbrook had served this function back in Roman times. Through the throng of the bar: the leather jackets, the girls with their spiked hair, and the skinheads like himself, down to the band.

The stage was tiny and to your left as you entered. It took a minute or two for your eyes to adjust to the gloom, and for your ears to pitch to the loudness. People were chattering, ordering drinks and flirting. A song was playing, a real humdinger: 'Mucky Pup'... a punk record from local Essex Road boys, Puncture. Yep, there were a lot of mucky pups here alright, and like the tension in the fast-paced punk rock, all looking for a release. The band hadn't started yet; people were settling in and getting drunk.

Then a riffle of drums, some toing and froing on stage, and all eyes turned. Some snaps of the snare and notes from the bass, and they were off. The front of the crowd started jumping straight away. There was a lot of teenage boredom to let loose. Teenage boredom and speed. Joe wasn't one for the crush, not with decent shmatta on at least, so hung back and finished his pint.

The band were good. Fast, tight, and a dynamic singer with a captivating pair of eyes. The more they played the deeper he was pulled into them. She was wrapped in a crazy dress that was more of a robe and her head was framed in lace with long pigtails hanging either side. The more she committed to the music, the faster the pigtails whipped around her head. She held the stage. Her dancing was angular and she used all the small amount of stage space to magnify the pulse of the music with her presence.

Those eyes, though. Lene Lovich had ethereal eyes. Eyes akin to Le Fanu's *In A Glass Darkly* laid open on a nightstand. With the beer running through him, not enough that he needed a piss but enough that he was feeling his swagger, with the stomp of the music and the pull of those eyes, he elbowed his way through the densely packed crowd to the scrum at the front. He started jumping, losing himself and becoming part of the mob. They'd reached boiling point and were ready to roll out of the saucepan of Friday night. The next song started with a high-pitched wail, the keyboards hummed and the pressure built to a steady beat. From the opening low throb of the keyboard he knew the song. It was his favourite of the band's: 'Bird Song'. Lene Lovich prowled the front of the stage, sweat streaming from the enraptured crush, and then, as she struck a pose, arms akimbo, they were up and on the minute stage and in with the band.

It was joyous, ecstatic, Dionysian even. They'd been longing for this release all week. Keeping it clenched inside them from teachers, bosses, and dole queue clerks all week. Now it was finally their turn. Joe was up on the stage, jumping in time to the pulse of the music with the rest of them. He was next to Lene Lovich, who was still singing, and dancing herself. Close up she was even more fascinating. Her eyes said so much, only Joe couldn't work out what the language was, he just knew what they were saying. She was doing a dance in front of him, bobbing up and down. He was facing her, drawn in, and moved to wrap his arms around her and plant a kiss. She was having none though; her eyes flashed and she took a bite of his cheek. The sheer shock of it sent him reeling back as she swirled away into the throng and people cleared the stage for the next song.

In a daze Joe stood to the side and dabbed his cheek. There was a sticky red and salty sweat; it stung. There was blood – not much but blood all the same. Red, krovvy, claret.

He wasn't too pleased, but he'd had far worse of a Friday night. It was nowhere near as bad a pasting as the Gooners might administer. Fuck it, he rubbed his cheek and moved back to the bar. At least he'd have a story.

As he handed over money in exchange for a lager top, that cockney nod to sophistication, he caught a glimpse of himself in the mirror behind the bar. On his cheek, on the left-hand side of his face, the bite resembled a red downturned mouth, just above and to the left of his bigger downturned mouth. The sight caught him as funny; it didn't hurt much, the adrenalin was still pumping, but the sweat running into it made the wound sing, and there was enjoyment to that song too. He thought of the bite and thought back to those eyes.

CHAPTER 2

Reynolds was a cold person. He didn't feel that himself of course; oh no, he was above that and that's where the coldness lay rooted. He never had got on with other people. He saw them as pawns on a chessboard. He scraped to the bigger pieces, but was looking to use them either by obsequiousness or, at the moment they started to topple, by adding a push. Suffice to say he'd been a prefect at school.

Girls were a problem, and at the same time no problem. Whilst he couldn't talk to them as people or get them to like him as himself, the fact that he was already a managing director made sure that those who were blinded by his position, or calculating enough to see him for what he was and play him for it, fell his way. One of those wankers that couldn't chat up a girl in a pub but would always be in the stationery cupboard with a temp after promising her the earth, or a full-time job at least.

This particular night he'd been out with some of the management from the job. In the City, that part of London where no one really lives but so many lives are ruined. He'd laughed at the right jokes, bought the right people the right drinks. It wasn't a night out with colleagues for him; it was a ladder he was climbing. Sometimes the snake is on the ladder.

The glow of the red wine he'd been drinking brought some colour to his pallid cheeks at least. He was making for Liverpool Street and the train that'd take him back to his suburban flat.

As he strode the tumble of building works that were making up the Barbican out of bomb sites, he heard a soft step behind him. The tread got heavier as it approached and then sped up. Reynolds quickened his gait but the following steps got faster yet.

He turned and caught a quick glimpse of a red gingham-checked button-down shirt and an overly hirsute, snarling face. The eyes seemed to flash amber, and the fire in the amber made him piss yellow as he broke into a run.

It wasn't just the eyes; the snarling mouth had sharp pointed teeth. Sharp pointed teeth that weren't natural to a man, and this man did not look anything natural. Cold piss ran down his leg and his trousers clung to him as he ran.

He didn't get far. He was caught by the back of the collar and pulled forcibly back by one quick tug. He dropped heavily onto his back. He wheedled on the ground, Kafka's cockroach, but with less dignity as his arms and legs were wheeling six times as fast. He suddenly reeled in pain as three sharp kicks danced into his ribs, knocking the air from his lungs. He tried to scream but there was no breath to do so. The sound the kicks made as they landed was akin to a baby taking a shit. He flung his hands to his face and tried to curl but his assailant was upon him. All breath seized as the teeth found his neck, tore at his throat and then the blood began to pour.

East London streets see more than their fair share of piss and shit and blood, and now Reynolds was part of it.

CHAPTER 3

Already opening time and Joe was hurrying on from work. It had been a long shift of printing the news, news that other people made. The world turned with the rich and famous parading the ease they moved through it. For all the strikes and wars and bovver the world never seemed to turn over so the likes of Joe got any comfort. The massive print rollers moved and you could be crushed by the world or move with it.

He was thirsty and was going to meet some mates in the Butcher's Arms. Some of 'em were on the print like himself and others were in Smithfield meat market. The lads here worked hard and could drink well. Round Farringdon and Clerkenwell many of the pubs had early and late opening for the trades. To get a pint you had to have either ink or blood on you, staining your clothes or colouring your thumb. Back in the '50s the Butcher's boasted it was 'London's only pub in the middle of the road', and sure enough, it was on a fork in the road, built directly over the Metropolitan Line so that when a tube passed under the whole pub rumbled, right down to the bricks it rested on.

Coming from work he didn't have his best gear on, but all the same he didn't look a nebbish. Red gingham Brutus button-down, 501s held up with quarter-inch braces, cherry red eight-hole Martens with an antique polish and a beige 'arrington. There was a badge pinned to each collar of his jacket; on the left a green one that stated in white letters 'Ere we go 2-3-4'. That being cos it was the shoulder he led with in a barney and cos it was a line from 'Jilted John'. On the right sat a Misty in Roots badge, them being one of the better British reggae bands. He'd seen 'em several times. Put all that with his tram-lined number four crop and a love of reggae and football and it spelt 'skinhead'.

Joe was happy as you could be at work; many people weren't, or even in work. Times were getting savage. At least he had a trade, print, and worked with people like himself. Yeah, you worked for a boss, but the union was strong and what that meant was togetherness and people took more than a paltry wage home. To Joe the tall blocks of offices springing up around the city isolated and crushed.

He cut a swagger up the Farringdon Road, thumbs in his belt loops. He was hoping to get to the pub before any of his mates so that should there be any office girls he'd have first crack at them. As usual he'd probably get knocked back in no uncertain terms, but at least it wouldn't be in front of his mates. He also knew Friday kicked off the weekend, and who knows? Nothing ventured, nothing gained.

There was a smattering of people in the pub. The *Guardian* building was opposite and there were several printers and typists in. He moved to the bar and ordered his usual lager top, his first pint of the weekend. After a day surrounded by the noise and heat of printing presses it was welcome. He basked in the relative quiet of people chatting. One bloke in a turtleneck and brown leather *Sweeney* coat was holding forth about how much he loved Chelsea. Joe cast his eye around the bar, hoping to see a girl he fancied. Though there were a few lookers in, there was nothing about them that interested him. They were just straights – none of 'em would be able to discuss the merits of the latest Joe Gibbs sevens, and would even less appreciate the antique shine of his Docs. Oh well, he'd be at a gig tomorrow night that'd be packed with skinheads, mods and punks, much more his type.

He'd downed his pint and was ordering another when a voice over his shoulder bellowed: 'Make that two!'

He knew the voice and turned his head to the right and looked over his shoulder to his mate Dennis and gave him a familiar 'Wotcher.'

Two pints it was and with them in hand they

moved to the back of the pub, close to the door. A good spot to see without being seen.

Dennis was an energetic lad. They were the same age and both from Hackney. They'd gone to different schools but were both well into reggae music and kung fu films. Dennis had an ear for the punk bands too. Joe less so, but he was also of an opinion that were enough bad things in life that you should say yes to anything even a little bit good.

Behind his spectacles Dennis made an enquiring face and poked his finger into the fading bite mark on Joe's left cheek. 'What happened 'ere?'

'I was at a Lene Lovich gig last week. She bit me,' Joe replied flatly, knowing some quip would follow. And sure enough:

'That wasn't very lucky, was it?'

Joe gave a pained look. 'It's not a permanent.'

'She's spooky that one,' Dennis continued. '"The framework is all right at least. I can see that, and pented black–" That how it was?'

Joe shook his head and with a pained look said, 'There's an Oliphant in the room.' Wanting to change the subject he asked: 'What's on for the weekend?'

'The Ruts!' Dennis replied excitedly.

'The Ruts...' Joe pondered and then 'The Ruts,' they both agreed, nodding their heads and then sipping their pints.

The Ruts were damn good punk rock. They were

a good band, whatever style you wanted to paint 'em in. Many of the punk bands were hollow fashion mannequins but The Ruts had something to say and sounded brilliant saying it. There was space to their music, a dub-like separation between the instruments that heightened their intensity. The band were reggae fans, and mates with Misty in Roots – it showed in the spark and direction of their songs. They were top notch live too.

Anyways, a decent band playing live also meant drinks and girls, and that he considered was surely no bad thing. What was, though, was that he'd only had a few pints and wasn't exactly feeling match fit. Nothing that bad, just a sense of unease, and he was itching. Weird, but the sides of his face, down the hairline, were itching. He scratched but the itch didn't go away. It was strange but he thought it was probably just dust from the printshop.

Dennis was still on about The Ruts, that and an Angela Mao film he'd seen recently, *The Legendary Strike*. He was pretty excited because Carter Wong was also in it. Angela Mao was one of their favourite kung fu stars – she was as focused as she was cool.

'Yeah mate, she was top drawer in *Bandits, Prostitutes and Silver*. Them little spinning metal discs in shoes she uses to cut people with when she fights were the business,' Joe chipped in.

'Know what was unusual about that film?' asked Dennis.

'The director mate,' Joe said. 'Kao Pao-shu. Not too many kung fu films directed by women.'

'Look mate, I ain't feeling so good. I'm gonna chip and I'll catch you tomorrow.'

Dennis nodded. 'Okay, you must be grim, you're leaving half a pint.'

That was a sorry state of affairs but by now Joe's stomach was flipping, and that itch wasn't any better either.

He left the pub to get the bus up from Clerkenwell Road. Come morning he remembered all that and he remembered scraping at stubble in front of his ears. Weird that. He recalled that and feeling queasy and nothing else of the night.

CHAPTER 4

Inside the hall a band was already playing. They were the first band on so no one was bothered or paying them any attention. All the same the thud of the bass was working its way into the beat of everyone's pulse and the snap of the drums was getting the odd head nodding.

Excitement cloyed the air. It hung heavy, the air hazy like petrol fumes. It only takes a spark to ignite petrol and it's the same with excitement. The tension waiting for it to happen was palpable.

The venue was close and hot. Youths crowded the bar and dance floor, drunk on Friday night and high on youth. A punk with a shock of white, spiky hair in bright trousers and a Dennis the Menace jumper was moving between knots of people touting his *Ripped & Torn* 'zine. A couple of punk girls bought copies and a rotund skinhead snarled as the zinester approached; the punk swerved to another gaggle of leather jackets. It was the weekend – muscles were flexing, drinks were flowing, blood was pumping.

The skinheads were, inevitably, crowding the

bar. Crews from different parts of town were eyeing each other uneasily; a company of wolves, indeed. The odd punk would accidentally get between the groups and blunder into a skinhead, then get a slap and skitter off quickly. As a result the floor was getting sticky as their spilled beer soaked into the layer of dirt trod into the cheap carpet.

Joe was into his second pint with one of his mates, Flipper. His real name was Philip and he was a short Irish lad that lived on the manor. He was over from Ireland to work on the building sites and had a love of good music and cheap beer. A good lad, everyone agreed. He was sporting 501s, a Celtic football shirt and a pair of sturdy brogues. He was midway through a long, rambling joke when a couple of skinhead sorts walked slowly past the pair.

One in a tight Union Jack t-shirt, short denim skirt and cherry red monkey boots definitely gave Joe the eye. Union Jack t-shirts were often, but not always, a sign to Dodgy Town, but when it was filled this well he thought he'd chance it. He smiled at her and saluted her with his pint.

'Wotcher,' he proffered.

'Oh, alwight,' she replied.

'Who're you then?'

'They calls me Mungo.'

He chuckled inside – named after a cartoon dog. Probably best not to mention it he thought. He gave her both their names. Her mate whispered to Mungo and then turned away to look to the other side of the room.

'She says you two are both 'ackney,' Mungo blurted.

Stamford Hill where he was from was more of a village to tell the truth, or shtetl given how Jewish the area was, but it was part of the London Borough of Hackney, so she had it close enough. 'And?'

'Bit of a "mixed" mob, innit?'

And there it was. All too obvious what the Union Jack t-shirt was saying now.

'And that's how we like it,' Joe stated firmly.

'It just ain't proper,' she taunted.

Joe was bored that someone who looked a sort was such an idiot. He was losing interest in her but thought he'd up the game as he'd nothing to lose and now took a pop at her denim skirt and a t-shirt less than style.

'If you was proper skinhead you'd be better turned out than that.'

'I'm wearing suspenders though!' she said and flipped the hem of her skirt up to give him an eyeful.

Sure enough, she was. Peach knickers too, that was a turn-up. With that she wandered off to the other side of the bar and to a large mob of cropheads.

The lads turned back to the bar and Flipper pressed on with his joke.

Twenty minutes later, still in the crush at the bar, he felt a rub to his elbow. She was back. She took Joe's pint from his hand, took a sip and gave it back.

'That's my boyfriend over there,' she said with a toss of her head to the other side of the room.

'So I suppose a nosh is out of the question?' Joe put out there.

'No,' she giggled. 'Quick, upstairs.'

Flipper's jaw dropped and Joe and the sort were traipsing up the mess of the stairs to the toilets. Salubrious they weren't. The grime was of the ultimate kind which you could write your name in. Graffiti covered the walls; bands and obscenities, sometimes both. Spattered amongst them were football teams and who'd done what to who.

Pushing the door – emblazoned with a huge pair of crossed hammers – open, Mungo strode purposely to one of the stalls. As she strutted through, the row of lads standing pissing in the stained ceramic urinal were shouting: 'Oi Oi!', ''ave a word!' One genteel punk was trying to push his dick into his faded combat trousers but couldn't stop pissing. Following close behind, Joe shut the door behind himself and turned the lock.

She leant forward and stuck her tongue into his mouth forcefully, then she stepped back and whipped her t-shirt up and over her head. She kept it tight in her left hand as if she was worried he'd grab it and make a run for it which, to be fair, had crossed his mind.

He looked down at her pale breasts. They were crammed forcefully up in a peach M&S bra. Why is M&S underwear so ubiquitous? He rubbed his finger around her left nipple, feeling the soft sheen of the material. Then he slid his hand inside and lifted the breast free. As he was doing so she reached behind herself and tipped the lid of the loo shut whilst unzipping his fly with the other hand. As his cock popped out blindly into the world she sat down and undid her bra; it dropped into her lap. Her right hand then reached over to his cock and wrapped itself firmly around it, giving it three quick pumps.

He looked down and saw her handiwork. The India ink DC spot tattooed at the base of her forefinger and thumb looked back up at him. Right now it was the omphalos around which his world spun.

She swirled his cock clockwise between her breasts, which swung slightly to the left and right, and then he felt the warmth of her mouth as she closed it around his member and started to ease it back and forth, slowly picking up speed. He shut his eyes and leant slightly back. Through the floor he could hear the band starting and the amplified words of the surly Sunderland singer. He was yelling about being wound up like a clockwork orange. Joe was feeling that alright.

She was getting faster and faster and the pressure to release had Joe curling his toes, not easy inside spit-shined Frank Wright loafers. As his wet spurted into her mouth he said 'You... know... I'm... Jewish?' in between deep heaves of breath. Her eyes widened as though she'd unexpectedly filled her knickers. He stepped back quickly, zipped and hastily got out of there. Flipper was there by the pishers, jaw still at half mast, and they both walked briskly down to see what they could of the band.

Clocking them as they came back into the hall was a burly bloke with big sideburns and a tatty England football scarf tied at his neck, replete with the spatters of faded brown bloodstains. He'd been at the other end of the bar earlier and he didn't look best pleased.

CHAPTER 5

The ivy grows thick in Abney Park cemetery. It wraps itself around the trees and monuments and obscures them, much as the stories and legends obscure the mysteries of London. The gravestones heave up from the ground like the teeth of a badly dentisted but black-haired and winsome girl. The cemetery is wild. It's long been so. After dark it's a home for creeping things and things that creep. Come darkness it's a trysting place. Some deliberately seek the dark, as there is no love in what they do; others are forced into the shadows by a harsh world that despises their love. All performed amidst the gravestones as the Salvationists buried beneath moulder. In the words of ghetto poet Israel Zangwill: 'There was an indefinable melancholy about the sere landscape. Russet refuse strewed the paths, and the gaunt trees waved fleshless arms in the breeze...'

It was a crisp morning. The innumerable birds were singing. Isn't that the true savagery of nature: it just goes on?

WPC Bittner was taking down a witness

statement. It was starting out to be a beautiful day, but now it was mired in sanguine horror. Two bodies, savagely killed, and a witness traumatised further by having to relive the events to a tired and calloused police force.

She was tall, lithe, and pretty. Her good looks led people to underestimate how clever she was, yet she wasn't as clever as she thought she was. She'd learnt from school and university to ignore those beneath her and to sycophant to those higher. She knew that people reacted to her on the basis of her appealing face: though she didn't like it, she knew it happened.

One of the reasons she'd joined the Met was so that she could become nondescript in uniform. What she hadn't counted on was that many men just saw the uniform as a challenge and that it acted as a backdrop to her looks rather than a cover. The deep blue set off her eyes and the blonde of her hair; her height was accentuated by the hostess-style hat which did nothing for authority; and the black stockings and sensible shoes actually brought to attention her long, shapely legs. All the same, she had a sharpness of mind and could use the fact that she was stereotyped to her advantage if she'd the confidence. Practically all her arrests got a crude snigger whenever she cautioned 'Anything you do say will be taken down...'

A phone call had come into the station and Bittner and another PC were directed to see what the incident was. The caller wasn't clear. He could have been drunk, high, or just a weirdo. A combination of all was also possible. On arrival outside the cemetery the caller was waiting by the phone box he'd called from. He was trembling and ashen. He stuttered out that there were people dead in the cemetery, two people, he'd seen them be attacked and ran for help once he thought it safe to do so. He was reluctant to go back into the cemetery. Bittner was soothing and said he'd be safe with the two constables. The male PC was firmer and grabbed the man by the shoulder and directed him to take them to the site of whatever had happened. They had to scramble over the wall. Although the cemetery had its fair share of nocturnal perambulations, the gates were locked.

Going through the pockets of two corpses at the base of a gravestone trying to glean who they were wasn't exactly detective work, but it was better than telling off kids and directing traffic. The bodies were of a man and a woman – both were battered and torn. Their faces were distorted both by bruises and by a look of sheer terror, frozen at the point of dying. They'd been beaten so badly that the partial tread of soles was livid on their bodies. Bittner made sure to make note of that, and drew a sketch of the imprint even before the police crime-scene photographer had arrived to set about his task. It wouldn't be a pleasant one – half of the man's face had been crushed, the eye socket was broken and his teeth were visible through tears torn into his bloody cheek. Already the blood was cloyed with the murk of death.

She'd gone through the pockets of the man first. Men tended to carry more on their person; women preferred a handbag. There was none such near the bodies but there would be a search for one. There was a fair amount of money in the man's pockets. That took robbery away as a motive. There were also the expected keys in his front pocket, wallet on his hip, and interestingly a worn wedding ring in the tight ticket pocket of his jeans. That told a story in itself, but what it was and how it related to the dead woman next to him remained to be unravelled. The woman's pockets revealed little other than money and a Spangles wrapper. Cola.

Before doing this she'd spoken to the witness. He was hysterical, frightened and clearly worried. Both he and Bittner knew he'd been 'cruising'. She didn't care about that, but he was clearly frightened that the police, as they were prone to, would make much of it. She'd done her best to calm him, and led him by suggesting he was 'out for a walk' before asking what he'd seen…

'Yes. Yes, I was out for a walk,' he whispered. 'Out for a walk when I saw the couple in front of me. I was resting, on a bench. Hand in hand they were. They were on the path, walked past me and up to the fork. That… that's when it happened.'

The only sound was his heavy breathing, the

rustling of the PC searching the undergrowth, and the rasp of the pencil on Bittner's notebook. She had to be careful as to what she wrote. Her posh upbringing and schooling meant she found accents very difficult. In Berkshire and Surrey she'd be fine, but it was something of a standing joke about her and cockney accents back at the police station.

'He just tore into them, both. Tore into them and knocked them flat. Then he was on them...'

'Who?' she prompted. 'Did you see who it was?'

'Just from behind. He was big, a burly brute.'

'And what did he look like?'

'It was all a blur. Fast, so fast. His face was a snarl, and it was hairy. I didn't get a clear look. He was wearing a checked shirt, and braces. I could see them from the back of him. Braces... and boots. The boots, he stamped on them... over and over.'

'Are you sure?' she queried.

'Yes, the moon was up. A full moon it was. I saw clearly but it was fast. So, so fast.'

He was starting to shake again and she placed her hand on his upper arm to calm him. He could give a more detailed statement back at the station, she had enough for her initial report: a man and a woman, the wedding ring, a bit of a description. The clothing was certainly distinctive, skinhead gear. Any copper in London knew that. The sketch she'd made of the prints on the body, she wondered if they'd lead to a particular pair of boots. The location? Ah yes, right next to the grave of George Leybourne, with the carved epitaph 'God's finger touched him and he slept.'

Joe was up late. He was putting on a clean shirt and caught sight of himself in the wardrobe mirror. It looked as though his sideburns were growing in thicker, and despite being cut a fortnight back his hair was looking shaggy. For no good reason that he could discern, he started to sing: 'Champagne Charlie is my name. Champagne drinking is my game. Good for any game at night my boys. Good for any game at night my boys…'

CHAPTER 6

Kippers stared up at him from dark toast, their golden hue contrasting with the drab streets outside. A mug of lukewarm char and two bottles of relish also graced Joe's breakfast table. Num-numo was the relish he dolloped onto the side of his plate. 'What a bloody breakfast!' he swore. When he'd been living with his mum, dad and sister, meals had been much better, but on starting work he'd got his own place and was fending for himself, even over his gas cooker. Kippers at least were a doddle to cook. They didn't 'alf pen and ink though. He opened a window before leaving, hoping the bedsit wouldn't smell of fish by the time he got back.

This morning Joe wasn't feeling match fit. He had been boozing last night and had a bit of a head, to put it mildly. He remembered having some beers, but not much thereafter. He must have done something: his jeans and Martens were filthy. There was thick mud, and what looked like claret, spattered over 'em. He definitely didn't remember having a row but it wasn't impossible of a Saturday night; it's alright for fighting, after all. He'd stick 'em in the laundry later, and give the boots a polish. Mud? Where'd he been? The only mud he normally saw was at Brisbane Road or Hackney Marshes, and that was with a game of football on it.

It was usually Brick Lane of a Sunday. Market is too glamorous a word, but you could buy most anything there, dirt cheap an' all, and there was no shortage of dirt. Half of the market was local dossers each with a blanket spread on the ground upon which they'd place their wares. These could be anything: a toothbrush, a couple of 'worn' porn mags, a spark plug, and some random tzatzke. An enterprising young chelloveck could pick up some decent soul and reggae records there, quite often some decent button-down shirts, and the odd Crombie or sheepskin too. His dad had long reckoned you could buy the whole market for a score. A lad like Joe, he'd pick up some bits and pieces for himself and some things he could punt on at Camden Market to the trendy punk rockers that steered clear of the East End and were used to paying more.

As such it paid to get there early; there was still good stuff to be found. Also he could clock the regular National Front paper sale at the top of the market. Not that he'd ever buy any of their drek but he could see who was there. He'd had run-ins with a few of the gumby skinhead types that hung out there and he liked to know who was about rather than bump into them unawares. A lot of skinheads were under the sway of Derrick Day, a hard, scar-faced brawler who actually held some respect. He'd kept his daughter out of secondary school for over a year, saying he didn't want her contaminated by mixing with other races and red teachers. Joe was amused as his dad was a full-on trade unionist and red and had no time for teachers. The Bovshovers had been amongst the people organised by Rudolf Rocker, the syndicalist, in the East End during the 1900s. The full-time Fronters were anoraks with a touch of something unsavoury about them. Day was local, shouted the odds and backed it up. Racists from out of London in particular used to come in by train to Liverpool Street on a Sunday and swagger around Brick Lane. It's said that most of us live on the crumbs that fall from the rich man's table; these were those who fought over the crumbs rather than the cake.

Still not feeling his best, Joe thought something to eat might steel him. Sat at the top of the Lane was the beigel shop. It never shut and was never quiet. Joe joined the busy queue that was already swathed in steam from the beigels being boiled at the back. He'd been there a minute or two when Matt Worley bowled in, one of the lads that Joe often went to gigs with. Another crophead youth. He was keen on fanzines, which Joe liked about him, but also Adam and the Ants, which Joe didn't. He usually had a fanzine stuck in his hand or back pocket. 'The most basic form of democracy,' he'd say about fanzines. Interesting enough the first time you heard it, but it had got to be a bit of a lecture and Joe had heard it way too many times. As per, he was sickeningly chipper: 'Wotcher.'

'Alright,' Joe replied. He saw that Matt had a battered sports bag with him. 'Snagged anything good?'

'Yeah mate, *Otis Blue*, *Hot Numbers Vol. 2*, some Pama sevens, and a couple of Pan horror story books.'

An impressive haul indeed. Matt produced the vinyl from the bag, a couple of Derrick Morgan singles on Crab, a Max Romeo on Unity, and on Camel he had the Hippy Boys' 'Cat Nip', which was easily the pick of the bunch. There was also a bag of broken biscuits which you'd get for cheap at most East End street markets.

Whilst they were queuing for their beigels, chopped herring for Joe, lox and cheese for Matt, they took in the full beauty of the *Hot Numbers* cover. A pneumatic sort was sat, legs akimbo, wearing high boots and very short shorts on a grassy slope. The temperature in the already steamy shop went up a notch.

'So Kessler's little mob were asking after you,' Matt put in.

'Me?'

'Well, someone's been troubling Kessler's bird. They didn't say it was you, and I don't think they know it was you, but they're after some agg. I'd keep 'em guessing, mate.'

'Me? You sure?'

'That wasn't you gettin' a nosh at the Upstarts then?'

Joe turned a half dozen shades scarlet. 'Yeah, it was. How'd they know it was me?'

'They don't,' Matt laughed. 'But that bird's got a shiner and her bloke ain't best pleased. Someone's gonna get a shoeing, and the geezer is siiiize of an ox.' Matt laid that on thick, opening his arms to show how big the bloke was and doing the voice from the Banana Splits cartoon where one of the Arabian Knights could transform into any animal simply by saying 'Size of a...'

'He'll get the size of my boot up his arse,' countered Joe, if a little uncertainly. This was more than he'd thought likely and he could certainly do without. Kessler was a git. He called himself Kessler cos it was the name of a writer who wrote a series of trashy novels about the SS. They weren't as good as Sven Hassel's; the git hadn't even gone for the name of the war-story writer people actually appreciated. He would be a problem – he was a nasty piece of work and a big piece at that. He bowled around with a cheap England scarf round his neck, winter and summer, and never cleaned the thing. Tawdry. It seemed what Joe had got up to with Mungo was being bruited.

With beigels in hand the lads went their separate

ways. Joe took a right, away from the master race's paper sale, past the equally sad commie one, and down towards Cheshire Street on the left. The Lane was long and grey; it was lively and the East End rubbed shoulders along it. As always it was full of people, all sorts of people.

Bustling through the crowd towards him he clocked a skinhead he didn't know giving him an intense stare. The lad was elbowing people aside and keeping his eyes firmly locked on Joe's. Tucking the beigel he'd been chomping into the pocket of his 'arrington he let his arms drop to his side, fists balled, ready for whatever might happen. He remembered what young Alf relates in Clarence Rook's *The Hooligan Nights*: 'I've 'ad a good many scraps in me time, nor it wouldn't seprise me if I was to have some more.'

Sure enough, the lad made straight for Joe.

'Didn't I see you at the Upstarts last week?' he questioned, with more than an edge of threat to it.

'I was there, didn't see you,' Joe replied.

'We saw you,' and the lad swung.

Joe had been expecting it and easily stepped back. A swing took time landing and was a clumsy opening punch. Once the arc of the swing had bypassed him, Joe stepped forward and jabbed twice left and then a harder right onto the lad's nose, which folded the way a pair of M&S knickers do when they hit the floor. Blood streamed down his face and splashed onto his grey Lonsdale t-shirt. Whilst the lad was still stunned and blinking the confusion from his eyes, Joe nipped around him and walked briskly through the crowd. He didn't run, he knew that'd draw attention. He wasn't worried about the police – this was East London, no one was going to bother with them. But this lad would have mates not far away around the corner and they could bring a lot of bovver.

CHAPTER 7

Joyce and Ingrid, punk rockers both, were in the pub of a Sunday afternoon because they really couldn't think of anything better to do. They'd been over to Camden Market but there wasn't much happening there so had ended up back in Stamford Hill after an hour on the 253 spent talking clothes, music, and boys. They'd come in for a drink because there was no real reason to go home and, who knows, in a pub something might possibly happen?

Joyce had already sprinted into the toilets and changed from her worn army shirt into the new day-glo leopard-print t-shirt she'd got at Camden. Ingrid was left at the bar – all she'd got was an Undertones badge which was already pinned to the lapel of her leather jacket.

The pub was pretty much a wash-out. There were a load of old people supping on pints and port and lemons. The only thing of interest was two lads sat in the corner in an animated conversation. One was a skinhead type and he was chatting to another lad, dressed pretty much the same but with his hair just starting to tuft to dreads and sporting a pair of NHS specs.

Joe had decided to get away from Brick Lane quick when he'd given the skinhead a slap. He'd have mates very nearby, and they'd obviously now worked out it was him with Mungo at the gig.

He didn't bother with the train from Liverpool Street. It was close but there was a good chance he'd meet some dodgy types coming into the Last Resort shop from the wilds of Essex. That left the bus up to Stamford Hill – it'd run up Kingsland Road right past Hoxton but it was quick and some of the Hoxton lads were actually okay. The thing with Hoxton was if you got into a row there you'd end up fighting the whole estate.

He got to the 67 bus sharply over on the desolate Shoreditch High Street and rode it up through Dalston to Stamford Hill. He spotted Dennis going into the pub from the top deck of the bus, and then decided to follow him in. At least he was good for a laugh.

Ingrid could make out what the lads were talking about. The bespectacled lad was saying that Gordon Liu was the best kung fu actor, whilst the other was championing Angela Mao. She didn't really know who they were. She knew Bruce Lee

– everyone did – but she thought it was funny how passionate they were getting. Also, it was interesting that one of them was saying a woman was best. The seventies could end well after all.

As Joyce came back from the toilet and was strutting it to show off her new t-shirt the skinhead came up to the bar to order a couple more pints. Ingrid gave him a smile and he gave her a what he thought was subtle but wasn't once-over before paying attention to the badges on her lapel. There was that new Undertones one, a Stiff Records Ian Dury, and Steel Pulse. They seemed to get some approval as he nodded and said: 'Steel Pulse... nice.' Badges weren't only a statement of who you were but also a door to knock.

'I've seen 'em a few times,' she said. Like most punks she had a fair appreciation of reggae and Steel Pulse had been gigging solidly with punk bands with Rock Against Racism.

'I like 'em too,' the skinhead replied. She was quite hoping they'd get on. She liked the look of him, and the day had been boring enough already.

'Do you two want to come and sit with me and my mate?' he asked. 'We're quite harmless.'

Joyce leant in, 'I should 'ope so too. You 'eard? Couple of bodies they found in Abney Park this morning.'

'Bodies? In a cemetery?' he gave back with mock incredulity.

Ingrid was pleased to see he had a sense of

humour and gave his bicep a gentle tap with her fist, 'Oh you!'

They spent the afternoon talking, laughing and having a few drinks. The pub was on the corner of a side street and the busy main road going up Stamford Hill. It had large windows and even though evening was coming in it remained light.

Dennis was eager not to miss a Hammer film that was on TV and so was away home. He and Joe had been mates since school. He was a Clash fan and the energy of punk got him fired. Although he was pretty sure he'd end up in a dead-end job like most of the Hackney lads he was doing his best to rebel, find his own way and not end up signing on or watching the clock.

Ralph Bates was starring in the Hammer film. The Victorian toff look that actors like him had in the films was one the skinheads liked. Ralph Bates dressed distinctly. The skinheads sported cravats and Crombie coats with velvet collars in emulation.

Joyce was also off home; her mum was a terror apparently. Joe and Ingrid stayed to finish their drinks and then Ingrid said that she'd be going. Joe had taken a shine to her bright eyes and spiky black hair as well as her intelligence and sense of humour. Not a bad taste in music neither, he thought.

Ingrid lived with her mum, dad and sister not too far away, down on the other side of Stamford

Hill towards the River Lea. There were flats tucked away on the sharp hill with a triangle of pubs: the Robin Hood, the Woodman and the Anchor and Hope, which was a funny little pub right up to the water. In the sixties it had looked as if it was in the forties, now in the seventies it was as though it was the fifties. You wouldn't find it if you didn't know it was there, it was so tucked away. Round about it was known as the 'Wanker and Joke' but aside from the painful characters all pubs attract there were some diamonds. Like Joe, the landlord Les was even an Orient fan.

Partly because he was being a gent, and partly because he thought he might get somewhere, Joe offered to walk her home, 'what with all these bodies turning up an' all', as he'd put it. She was quite pleased he was; she could see he liked her, and she'd taken a liking to him too, plus there *were* bodies turning up.

They took a winding route through the back streets. By the time they'd reached the crest of the hill dusk was falling. It still wasn't too dark as the moon was as full as a Tighten Up album. Joe was feeling restless but put it down to him talking to a girl he fancied, and seemed to be getting somewhere with. Several times he stretched out his arms, which seemed to be aching for some reason. He pulled at his collar and did that shoulder roll and forward nod of the neck that all the young skinheads did, this time not for show but because his muscles seemed tense.

They reached Ingrid's door. He went in for a kiss but she back-stepped and laughed. She did lean in and give him a quick peck on the cheek, said 'Call me' and shut the door. She was pleased he'd gone in for a kiss, but they'd only just met. As he hadn't tried more, she'd like to see more of him. For a bad lad he seemed quite good, and for a good girl... well she wasn't always that good. But not on her doorstep.

Joe was on his way home, walking along the towpath, still feeling weird. The evening mist was rolling down the water like an advancing wall. Joe's stomach was turning flips; even his teeth seemed to itch. On either side of his face his weak teenage sideburns were filling in. The hairs were sprouting and growing. They were like the arms of drowning sailors reaching for help. He was nauseous, his head fuzzy. His whole body felt as though it was rippling. The muscles of his arms, legs, and face cramped and flexed. Sweat ran from him. His limbs filled, grew taught; the sleeve of his shirt barely contained his bicep, which was now furring with coarse hairs. They made a hirsute run down his arms, over his chest, and his now-arching back.

His eyes clouded then, as though a moon reflected on pools of brackish water, and a bright yellow shone forth. Eyes, not Joe's eyes, but eyes with a different knowledge altogether.

CHAPTER 8

Stamford Hill has always been a village, even now it's been swallowed up by the London Borough of Hackney. Not only is it a village in the midst of a city, it's on the edge of so many things. The numerous chassidim with their shtreimels and silk coats definitely set the area apart, and in a sartorial as well as frum manner. The geography leads to the edge of the pale. Abney Park cemetery, where the two bodies had been found, is London's largest unconsecrated graveyard, the resting place of nonconformists dating back to 1840. Many a strange and many a forward idea is interred there. There're the marshes. Hackney Marshes to the north, just across the canal, a desolate part of London. Stories and legends include a stranded Viking fleet, Dick Turpin revelling in the local hostelries, and bodies being dumped. The River Lea had been the border between King Alfred's Saxon kingdom of Wessex and the Danelaw of Essex. Borders, peripheries, transgressions.

It's no surprise then that the marshes attracted Ken Campbell. He was an actor and writer who sat on the edges of theatre. He had a lively intelligence that was equally delightful and annoying. His distinctive voice seemed to constantly be mocking, even when earnest. He never switched off. The eyes beneath his bushy eyebrows burned with a keen knowledge, and what he didn't know he wanted to find out about. He found people fascinating and would talk to anyone who sparked his interest. He was currently recognisable from appearing in tough writer G.F. Newman's TV series *Law and Order* as a conniving brief the year before. It'd been a popular series in East London as it gave a realistic picture of villains, bent coppers and the chicanery of the law. If Dixon had ever patrolled the streets of Dock Green those days were gone forever.

This evening Ken was out on the canal towpath, just on the fringe of Springfield Park, with a camera. He wanted to get some pictures of the full moon and some of branches dipping into the waters to use as backdrops for theatre that he was working on. It was dusk, the moon was full and the evening was none too dark. A line from Hester Holland's tale ran through his head as he gazed up at the wide sky: 'though it gave the sensation of vastness, there was no atmosphere of peace.' He could see the silhouette of a figure coming towards him, crouched over but moving quickly. Whilst it looked to be a person, the posture seemed to be that of someone doubled over with stomach pain.

Perhaps he was in need of a toilet? As he got nearer Ken could hear snarling coming from the figure, and see eyes piercing the gloom, eyes the colour of golden beryl that cut through the gloom as a knife. Ken stepped away from the edge of the water – he didn't like the look of this character. He clutched his camera so as to have a tight grip of it in case it was snatched. The figure indeed came closer, and the snarling rose in pitch. Frightened for himself, Ken lifted his camera and pressed the flash. There was a terrific burst of light and the person ran off, still snarling and still moving fast. Ken was scared – the hairs on the back of his neck were upright, as were those on his head, such as there were.

A day later, once he'd developed the picture, what he saw sent a chill through him. Though blurred there was clearly a face, a contorted face that appeared to be covered in hair with sharp pointed teeth grimacing to a snarl. There was the shoulder of a tank-top jumper, and the button-down collar of a windowpane check shirt.

To get to and from his bedsit to work, Joe took a 76 bus. He was lucky to be in work and on the print like his dad. All the same, it was hard work. All that hard work so the press baron bosses could lord it. Joe thought it was bizarre that the many people working on the presses could have a thundering voice, but the only one ever heard was that of the bosses. It was no accident that the printers were prone to making typos, so ears became arse, as a way of flicking the Vs when they needed to.

The year had started with what became known as the 'Winter of Discontent'. His dad had been on strike for six weeks. Times had been tough and there were power cuts and rubbish piled high on the streets as dustmen were also out on strike. Stoke Newington Common, just a few streets down from Joe's, was used as a rubbish dump by the council. Vermin were rampant. He couldn't help thinking of James Herbert's novel *The Rats*.

But on the print he was. It was just a small print shop where he could learn the trade before getting taken on somewhere bigger.

The problem with taking the bus was that it ran close to the NF's headquarters, the grandiosely named Excalibur House on Great Eastern Street. There was no danger of himself crossing the threshold but it did mean you might bump into the odd nutter on the bus, or a team of lads thinking you were a Fronter who then took umbrage. Whilst not averse to a row, it was a different matter being taken for one of those plums. Excalibur House was a place many of the out-of-London seagull-spotters visited and where several of the pubs that the lads he seemed to be up against might be drinking in before heading home to the sticks. The tube was there, and the bus/tube traffic brought up all sorts. They wouldn't be there of a morning, but come evening, as it was now, there was always that slight tingle of risk.

So it was that as the bus eased into City Road there was a clatter of feet coming up the stairs and talking loudly as their owners took seats on the bus. Joe was sat right at the back, on the left-hand side of the steps. You wouldn't really be seen there unless someone were walking back to alight from the bus. They sat one in front of the other, and the foremost turned to continue chatting to the other. Jean jackets, tatty denim (not even Levi's, Joe thought), but jean jackets nonetheless, one with a Nazi eagle sewn above the breast pocket. Two of 'em, loudmouths, but one more than he.

The lad facing back clocked Joe and gave a malicious grin. He tapped his mate on the arm and nodded. The other then turned. After a quick look at each other they started down the aisle of the bus towards Joe. 'Kessler wants a word with you,' they sneered. Already seeing how this would pan out, Joe was up and halfway down the stairs. The bus was still moving, turning from City Road and up New North Road. Just around the curve of the stair, Joe turned slightly. He put his shoulders to the back of the bus and anchored himself on it, sideways on to the stairs. He knew he couldn't fight both of them, but he could create a bottleneck and cork them up. Sure enough, they quickly came thundering down the stairs only to be pulled up short by himself being in the way. The first one tried to punch down, but had to lean at too sharp a downward angle and wobbled off balance. Joe threw up a couple of quick cracks, aiming for the lad's 'nads but only being able to land a couple on his thigh. Still, they were solid punches and would hurt. The two of them stepped back up the bus and started to kick down, clumsily because the one behind had his leg wrapped around the other so neither had any force. The first lad had a tasty pair of Frank Wright loafers on. Proper shoes and, usefully, slip on. As he tried to swing the heel of it into Joe's face, Joe reached up and seized the shoe with both hands. Pulling down and back at the same time, he managed to slip the loafer from its owner. This lemon even had Union Jack socks: what a loser. As the bus slowed for a bus stop, Joe turned and legged it quickly off the bus and up the street. He turned to watch the two of them tumble out of the bus, landing in a heap. The one with only the one shoe was incensed, and let fly a stream of invective which only served to make him look more ridiculous.

Within a week Ken Campbell's picture had been run in the *Hackney Gazette*. Having an eye for publicity, he'd also sent it to the *Fortean Times* – they'd be most interested in what appeared to be a fuzzy-faced creature roaming the city. Being a quarterly, the *Fortean Times* moved at a slower pace and so it'd take some time for discussion to take off there.

WPC Bittner read the local paper over a cuppa in the canteen. The picture caught her attention. Though blurred, it was disturbing, and the description was certainly of interest: 'tank-top jumper, and the button-down collar of a windowpane check shirt...' Skinhead clothes. The bruises on the bodies at the cemetery had proven to come from Doctor Martens boots as she'd suspected, and here again was a description of skinhead gear. Might there be a thread to follow? She made a note to look into this skinhead link. The next day she'd get to the newsagent and go through the music papers *Sounds* and *NME*. Being young she knew that lots of the kids read fanzines that really told you what was going on with music, clothes and fashion. Being a copper she had no idea where to get any, but she would investigate.

CHAPTER 9

Ingrid and Joe had been out for a drink a couple of times. They clearly liked each other but nothing had 'happened'. Joe was keen for it to do so. He thought she was too, but like many a young bloke he was nervous of being knocked back and of what she might think. He'd give it a few drinks but also knew drink isn't always good for one's 'ardour' so got anxious about that too. As for Ingrid, she was just waiting for him to make the first move. She would if he didn't do it soon. She'd seen plenty of Slits gigs and was not a typical girl.

This Saturday morning she was keen to get over to the Small Wonder record shop in Walthamstow. She still hadn't got Patrik Fitzgerald's single 'All Sewn Up', not like his earlier singles on the Small Wonder label, but on a major. Keeping it street level, Soo Catwoman had done the sleeve. The shop was a small one but bursting with punk records and attitude. The owner, Pete, would frequently laugh at people's bad taste if they asked about records he considered naff. She thought she'd be safe getting a Patrik Fitzgerald single and was keen to see what other delights were lurking there, maybe even The Lurkers themselves?

Joe was happy enough: the pie and mash shop on Walthamstow Market was proper, and Small Wonder had a decent amount of reggae too. The bus took a while to journey up Lea Bridge Road to Walthamstow, and they'd planned a walk back along the River Lea, past the football pitches, back towards Ingrid's, and over to the Anchor and Hope pub for a pint.

It had been a pleasant morning. Ingrid had picked up the record she wanted, as well as a 12' of Eddie Grant's 'Living on the Frontline', a defiantly eerie 12' 'Bela Lugosi's Dead' that had a really dubby lead-in, and a Menace single. Joe had double-doubled at the pie and mash. Now sat at the back of the bus, he had his arm around her as the early afternoon sun poured through the windows. Ingrid, sat in the corner, leant forward to open the window and Joe dropped his hand down to her arse and gave her left cheek a playful squeeze. He loved how she looked, radiant in the sun. Vernon Lee described well how he felt in her 1890 story 'The Phantom Lover': 'I don't believe, you know, that even the greatest painter can show what is the real beauty of a very beautiful woman in the ordinary sense: Titian's and Tintoretto's women must have been miles handsomer than they have made them. Something – and that the very essence – always escapes, perhaps because real beauty is as much a thing in time – a thing like music, a succession, a series – as in space.'

He was hoping they could move up a step from phone calls and smiles. He got a smile and as Ingrid sat back she turned slightly and kissed him. Joe's pulse doubled and he could feel his vitality coursing through him. Being lunchtime the bus wasn't very full – there were only a couple of pensioners sat near the front – so Joe kept kissing her harder and slipping his tongue into her wet mouth. She kissed back and wrapped her tongue agilely around his. He was starting to move his hand up between her t-shirt and leather jacket; she had her hand on the inside of his thigh, gently rubbing. He could feel himself stiffen when she pulled back and said 'our stop' and laughed. 'Bollocks,' thought Joe, knowing he'd have to walk the aisle of the bus with a stonking hard-on.

Still feeling somewhat abashed, but pleased his kisses had been requited, Joe took Ingrid's hand as they strolled alongside the river. At the first bridge they crossed from the Clapton side over to the marshes. Joe wanted to spend as much time as he could with her before a pint and getting her home, up by the Woodman pub, so a stroll around this far side of the river was welcome. Joe led the walk out past the football pitches – there were dozens of games being played – and into the edge of the reeds, or at least Ingrid didn't push to go anywhere else. Once in the reeds he sat down and pulled her down on top of him. She giggled and fell onto him, wrapping her arms around him. She met Joe's kisses and even let her hands wander. He did likewise and now they were on their sides, face to face, in a deep snog. The reeds rose rigid.

Joe slid his hand up inside her t-shirt. The warmth of her skin was exhilarating. He tentatively ran his thumb and forefinger around the underside of her bra. She didn't tell him to stop so he moved his hand slightly higher and cupped her breast, then moved his hand widdershins in a slow, rotary manner. She kissed him all the more and encouraged his hand, now slipped round her back, to try and undo the garment. First he fumbled, then he got flustered. Like most young men he didn't have a clue what he was doing. Knowing this and laughing, Ingrid rolled astride of him and sat upright; she pulled up her shirt and unclasped the M&S brassiere. Her breasts tumbled loose. She leant forward until Joe's face was in between them and gently rocked her hips left to right, grinding his growing erection and causing her attributes to sway across his face. The softness of them added to Joe's hardness. He tried to roll on top but she held his shoulder down and kept herself in the driving seat.

Suddenly Joe was seeing stars. From behind him and, because he was on his back, upside down, he could see in his swimming vision some pre-pubescent herbert who'd just bounced a football off his head turning and legging it after yelling: 'Oi mister! Get a room.'

Ingrid burst out laughing as Joe leapt up. Pulling his braces back over his shoulders, he started running after the whippersnapper. To start with his legs were still weak from being sat on by Ingrid, but he soon began to get into his stride. The kid was tearing off through the football pitches, turning back every twenty-five yards or so to shout back another mouthful of cheek. He knew he wasn't going to get caught.

Joe was reluctant to lose face in front of Ingrid, and all the lads playing football, by stopping running, even though he'd never catch up. Giving up and walking back would be just as humiliating so he kept on going.

He'd given up and was just running for show when his eye caught sight of something in a pile of jumpers and cardies piled up behind a goalpost; a tatty football scarf with faded red, white, and blue fringes. Could it be? Joe pulled it loose – it was a filthy England scarf. As he held it up there came a loud shout of 'Caaaaaannnnt!'. Looking up, Joe saw Kessler at the far end of the pitch in football shirt and ridiculous shorts running towards him. Joe laughed and started off in the other direction, towards the bridge. He had a huge head start and knew he was gonna run clear. He ran across the football pitches and across the bridge. Kessler pursued but was getting hoots of laughter from the other players. Once he reached the other side, Joe jogged then skipped as Kessler stayed on the far bank and yelled a tirade of abuse. Joe lifted the scarf above his head, swayed it from side to side and sang 'Ing-er-land, Ing-er-land, Ing-er-land'.

CHAPTER 10

Every time he rammed hard behind her Sophie Slaughter's eyes blurred. Her mouth hung open and she was making the most deliciously disgusting grunts to accompany the slap of his loins against her bare buttocks. Her blonde hair splashed into her face as he thrust himself home. With each clap of flesh his balls swung forward and kissed her somersaulting pussy. She wasn't thinking about the dole queue, dead-end northern towns, or 'Maggie Thatcher milk snatcher', she was just running up the hill of the energy building up in her body until she could fly from the peak of the collapsing volcano. Already her legs were starting to tremble and she had to cling tighter and tighter to the fence atop the sharp drop to the railway line beneath.

She'd left her small northern town the year before after reading about The Slits, The Adverts, Penetration, and women in bands standing up and speaking for themselves. As it was she was the talk of her home town, and not for the positive. The anarchy that punk offered was madly attractive and as soon as she'd saved a few quid she was off to London, and an audience she hoped would appreciate her with that money stuffed into the pocket of her school blazer. Only now there was a badge on that blazer stating, *shouting*, 'Oh Bondage Up Yours!'

Right now she was in the dark of Stoke Newington Common with some pissed punk she'd met in the Jolly Butchers. The length of him was solid and for now had erased past and future. There was just this now. And now she was on top of the moment and wanting it to last for as long as it could before, once again, mundanity prevailed. She pushed back, meeting his exertions and setting a pace all her own. She was racing closer and closer to climax. Suddenly there was a shriek. She thought he was letting loose his all but she couldn't feel his momentum or weight. She could still feel him jammed inside her but his hands on her hips weren't there, nor was the pressure of his lean, or the heat of his breath. She peered, bleary eyed, over her shoulder and he was on his back, howling, blood pumping from the torn slash where once his manhood had protruded. Someone, or something, was hunched over him slashing at him with claws. Claws!

Sophie sprinted away, or at least tried to. At her first step his severed member slipped from her arse. What had once stood proud now flopped flaccid, oozing blood, much like a teabag lifted from a stewed cup of tea. At her second step she caught her foot in the loop of her M&S peach knickers that still hung on the ankle of her right foot. She teetered then fell face first into grass rapidly soaking with blood. Whoever had attacked her paramour leapt forward, but her falling prostrate meant they flew over her. She could feel the sweep of their pass. With that she was up, screaming and off. Her lips were drained of their rosebud hue; her pale blue eyes took on an aspect of terror.

Sophie ran terrified towards the lights of the road that ran around the Common. There was no traffic but street lights illuminated the road. There was no sound save for her screams.

Bittner, like most of the station, had been half-expecting the call. There'd been murders in the cemetery on a full moon, and tonight was another. Arriving quickly on the scene once they'd received the panicked call from a house on the edge of the Common, she was detailed to take an initial statement from the terrified young woman who'd been involved.

By now Sophie had pulled her underwear up and was wrapped in a blanket. She was still stunned by what had happened and the wide, blue eyes that attracted so many a man were now all the wider and haunted by something she'd never forget.

Bittner looked her over, pulled the blanket aside and, although the girl was covered in blood, could see no injuries. 'You're safe now. We're with you,' she kept repeating, 'You're safe.' The girl's eyes stared straight ahead. She'd still not said a word. The alarm had been raised when she'd ran along the road screaming at the top of her voice.

Police were already going over the area. Torches, flashing lights, radio static… none of it helping to calm the victim of whatever had happened. They'd found the body. It was a mess. It was semi-clothed, trousers still around its ankles, and a gaping hole where the genitals should have been. The ground was sodden with blood. The face and arms had been slashed horrifically.

Bittner sat the girl down; a neighbour pushed a cup of tea into the girl's hand. Even at so traumatic a juncture, tea was a panacea. The heat of the mug in her hand seemed to bring the girl's attention to. Her eyes started to focus and she looked around her, down at the tea in front of her and then at WPC Bittner. 'You're okay. You're safe,' Bittner was still saying over and over. The girl gave a slight nod to acknowledge the words and Bittner tentatively asked her name.

'So… Sophie,' she whispered.

'Sophie?' queried Bittner, who had her notebook

in her hand but was looking into the girl's face to show her she was not alone and to establish some rapport.

'Yes,' the girl nodded. Bittner asked if she could remember what happened.

'It were 'orrible,' Sophie whispered, 'I didn't see much. 'E just came at us.'

'Did you see who it was? Did you know them?' the WPC quizzed.

'Fookin' 'orrible, never seen nowt like it.'

Sophie's Yorkshire accent wasn't helping Bittner any, but she wasn't going to relent from questioning the victim and missing a lead before the detectives arrived and took all the credit.

'It were like a fookin' wooluf, all hairy an' slavering, an' them fookin' claws... the claws!'

Bittner made sure to make note of everything. She'd thought there'd be obvious sex and robbery motives but it was starting to seem there were reasons unknown. She pressed Sophie to recall what her attacker had been wearing and carefully made note of the reply:

'Light trousers, I couldn't see the colour, and a button-down shirt with big checks. His face, he had hair all down it.'

'Anything else?' Bittner asked. 'Any small detail might help.'

'The shirt sleeves! They were short and had a V-cut vent to them, with a button either side. He were swinging his arms and slashing, I saw 'em.'

Another button-down check shirt – Bittner remembered this detail from the cemetery killings. 'Was he wearing boots? Boots and braces?'

'No, he had brogues on. I saw 'em when I fell and he leapt over me,' Sophie recalled. 'Braces… yes. He did wear braces.'

Not a complete match with the previous description but Bittner thought it enough to show a similarity. She left Sophie with the ambulance man and went to tell what she'd learnt to the arriving detectives.

They were not as impressed as she'd thought they'd be. When she told them the attacker was a hairy-faced skinhead some of them laughed to her face. Once word got round that the surviving victim was a northerner no one took Bittner seriously at all. All assumed she'd once again made a pig's ear of a statement from a witness with an accent. One of the DCs made a joke that they should send her back to Hendon to watch *Coronation Street* for a week. Bittner took their laughs, folded them over and over and swallowed them. From *Sounds*, which she'd now started reading every Thursday, she'd got an idea of the kind of music the skinheads liked. This was a lead she'd follow even if the 'lads' were too dense to see it. *Sounds*, she'd found, was written for, and by, yobs. The *NME* was for the kids who'd read Isaac Asimov at school. She'd stopped buying that. Bittner had been busily checking in the gig listings where bands were playing and getting a good idea of where large numbers of skinheads, and trouble, would be.

Above, the moon was obscured as a cloud crossed.

CHAPTER 11

The reggae record was talking about wolves and leopards trying to kill the sheep and the shepherd. Joe sang along with the Dennis Brown single gracing his record deck. He'd woken after sleeping late and feeling rough, but after a strong coffee was feeling more chipper. After watching *The Ipcress File* he paid more attention to proper coffee. He'd got a copy of *Len Deighton's Action Cookbook*. Like Harry Palmer he thought that working-class people should live well. He'd bought a Bialetti coffee maker from the local Italian deli, a bit fanciful but it made coffee with a kick. Len Deighton advised treating coffee like a luxury, making it carefully, serving it hot and not wasting it by making weak brews. Joe agreed wholeheartedly. He'd taken to the whole ritual of making espresso in the morning. With a couple of cups in him and a stack of reggae records playing he was feeling set for the day already. He looked over to the picture of Madeline Smith sat in its frame on the bookshelf by his bed and gave her a wink. She was in a resplendent pose, the sauce for comedy and horror films, a distinct British glamour. The British take on glamour has more than a hint of kitchen sink to it – that it's a glamour we just might reach, or see through, is what makes it real compared with the untouchable Hollywood fantasy. Joe was particularly fond of a scene in *The Vampire Lovers* where she was seduced by the imposing Ingrid Pitt. Say no more.

Yesterday's clothes were strewn about the bedsit floor. They looked to be a right mess too, again, more than the normal weekend doings. Joe wasn't adverse to a tear-up but he wasn't one of those two-pint bullies. There was blood on his shirt and trousers. He didn't remember a barney. The warm cheerfulness of Madeline Smith faded as a vague doubt suggested itself. Still, if something that bad had happened he'd know about it, right?

He scooped the clothes up and dumped them into a duffle bag for the laundrette. His brogues could do with a polish too; he'd do it later. For now he pulled on a pair of Levi 501s, with a quarter-inch turn-up sewn onto the hems. He tucked in a green, windowpane check Arnold Palmer shirt – he was well pleased with that particular shirt – green socks, laced-up antique polished cherry red Docs with yellow laces, and a black tank top over the shirt once he'd pulled his braces over his shoulders. Looking into the wardrobe mirror, he ran his hand over his head to smooth over his number four crop before cramming money into his right front pocket and his keys into the left. He blew a kiss at the picture of Madeline and was off out the door.

This Saturday he'd planned to meet Dennis at noon. They were going to check Count Shelley's Third World Records shop down on Stoke Newington Road. Staying local meant there was little chance of bumping into any of Kessler's mates. There was a Cornell Campbell tune he wanted to give a listen, and from there they'd most likely head up west to Daddy Kool, another reggae shop, but this one was on Hanway Street in Soho. It was run by a notoriously bad-tempered West Ham fan called Keith who seemed to delight in arguing, with anyone, over anything. Buying records there – and they had a top-drawer selection – and getting insulted by Keith was as much a reggae fan's rite of passage as their first kiss and first beer.

They'd had a good afternoon: he'd picked up Dillinger's 'I Thirst', a spaced-out workout on the My Conversation riddim, Cornell Campbell's 'Mash You Down' on a sweet Lord Koos 12', as well as Junior Murvin in top form on 'Cool Out Son' over Real Rock, and produced by his faves the Mighty Two on the buxom Heavy Duty label. He'd also grabbed a couple of singles for Ingrid: the Clash's *Cost of Living* EP, which was a belter, and the Flamin' Groovies doing 'Werewolves of London'. Dennis had some joy too with a great

DJ choon, 'Barnabas Collins' by Lone Ranger, plus Captain Sinbad's 'Pressure Rock' and LKJ's 'Want Fi Goh Rave', which led to the question of what to do that night.

It was a Saturday night so they chatted about what bands were playing that evening. Prince Far I was in town; he'd been putting out some killer singles on his Cry Tuff label. The Only Ones were gigging but Joe reckoned there'd be too many raincoats. Essential Logic – but Dennis said too many students. They both liked the idea of going to see Black Slate. They'd been seeing them live since the Rock Against Racism gigs in 1977. The Chords were also a possible, but there'd inevitably be rucks at that and so they settled on The Members.

The band had one of the better albums of 1979. As a result of that, and their solid gigging reputation, the gig was packed. Joe and Dennis were both there after dropping their records at home, having their tea, and getting changed. Dennis had his at home; Joe went to the café. The food was hot and cheap – old men sat pushing their food around their plates. Arsenal had won, so they'd something to celebrate. They'd sing over a few beers this evening. But whether the team won, lost or drew they were going nowhere. The moon waxes, the moon wanes. A few lines from Lola Ridge's poem *The Ghetto* came to Joe's mind as though the moon through cloud:

Nude glory of the moon!
That leaps like an athlete on the bosoms of the
young girls stripped of their linens;
Stroking their breasts that are smooth and cool as
mother-of-pearl
Till the nipples tingle and burn as though little lips
plucked at them.
They shudder and grow faint.
And their ears are filled as with a delirious
rhapsody,
That Life, like a drunken player,
Strikes out of their clear white bodies
As out of ivory keys.

Joe was happy that music and style got him beyond the nine to five. He liked to dress smart – it reminded the toffs that even though he was a worker he was as good as, better than, they.

Dennis was in beige cord Levi jacket and trousers, a white Fred Perry, and baseball boots. Joe had polished his brogues. They gleamed and the blakeys nailed to the heels and toes made sure he stepped loudly. He was in a pair of gold and green Tonik trousers and a navy blue large gingham Brutus button-down. He wanted to look good as Ingrid was also along with them. She'd made an effort too, and was rocking a PiL logo t-shirt, with her leather jacket over that. She had a short monochrome dogtooth skirt that accentuated the black of the jacket. Along with them were Paul Barratt, Adina, Matt, Chok, Little

Ian, Chris Low, cropped heads, 'arringtons, Levi jackets, boots and braces.

As the band came on the crew moved from the bar towards the stage. The Members' singer Nicky Tesco was resplendent in a leopard-skin jacket and the band quickly worked up a sweat, as did the crowd. The band played a magnificent mix of punk and reggae. It was something of a standard for punk bands to drop some reggae, and not all did it well. The Members felt reggae rather than fashioned it. Their punk numbers had an authentic kick to them. Their songs were evocative thumbnail sketches, they spared neither pathos nor humour. There was pogoing, there was skanking and the whole place was enjoying the night.

Already outside the gig police were pushing people about. Young punk rockers mostly. Stopping, searching, tripping them over, insulting and provoking. There'd been a couple of arrests. Now the crowd was piling out of the venue, the police were lined up on either side of the doors and yanking out anyone they didn't like the look of. Joe and his mob kept well together. They'd learnt from football how to react to the police. There was no love for them in East London, or the rest of London for that matter. Joe's Bundist grandfather still toasted by lifting his slivovitz and saying 'Daloy politsey' – down with the police.

CHAPTER 12

Out on the street it was getting rowdy. The police were pushing people towards the tube station, and pushing over anyone they didn't like the look of. The young punks and skinheads were getting riled, which is exactly what they wanted. Joe's mates, being East Londoners, knew how the police operated and so kept together; a big bunch would be too much trouble for them. Joe, however, had a few beers in him, and a girl to impress, always a dangerous combination. He saw one copper trip over a punk and stopped to give him a mouthful. The rest of his mates were in front of him and kept walking. As the police started to scoop up and arrest people, the crowd surged. The Members had a song called 'Don't Push' and a few in the mob started to sing it. Their anger brewed, bubbled, and boiled. As ever though, the police were better organised and better armed.

Fighting quickly broke out. Truncheons were swinging, boots kicking. Noses broke and blood ran. There was a crush as those trying to escape were caught up with those trying to get into the melee. Joe's mates, Ingrid included, had made a sensible break for the tube. He was caught in the crowd. The harder heads wanted to brawl, the fashionable were desperately scrambling to escape, to the tube, on passing buses, running.

Fists flew but inevitably the fight was quickly over. As some coppers went toe to toe, others scooped up the kids and roughly dumped them into the backs of vans. Other coppers made sure they stayed there, and relished the job of cracking down on elbows and legs. Joe was suddenly pulled back by the collar, a couple of buttons bursting from his shirt. In between two coppers with no room to swing a punch or break into a run, he was frogmarched to a waiting police van, lifted and thrown into the back. Before he could catch his breath other bodies started landing on top of him. He struggled to breathe; sweat started to pour as the heat of so many pressed bodies and raw panic ran down the metal walls of the van.

Outside, the moon was up. It had risen since he'd gone into the gig. The moon was shining high overhead, full. Its luminosity laving all the earth in unterrestrial radiance. August Derleth says as much in his story 'The Adventure of the Tottenham Werewolf'. The moon shines weaker in the city. The light of city fighting against darkness blots out the stars and diminishes the black of the night that lets the glory of the moon shine forth, but for all of that it is the only object seen in the sky, and fascinates all the more for it.

Enlightened England exults in its wonders but there are dead children for the bricks of St Pancras Station, the grind of the factory, the aching gaps between the ticks of the office clock. For all the twinkling glass, arrayed shop windows and social progress of London, the bristles protrude, the teeth bare and the skin slips to loose the beast.

Beneath the press of bodies, unseen, Joe's sideburns were thickening, the hairs twisting. The puny hairs on his chest darkened. His eyes glowed a bright yellow, his muscles writhed, hands flexed. Beneath the weight of desperation Joe struggled for breath, and life; the monster in him fought to live, and this monster lived to kill.

Above the heap of half a dozen youths one PC was stomping on them with his black Dr Martens whilst the other leant over them indiscriminately raining blows with his truncheon. Suddenly an arm shot through the writhing mass. It grabbed the copper leaning forward by the face, pulled him forward, and then raked his face. Sharp claws slid through the skin of the constable's face and blood spouted from the cuts. His nose was slivers flowering around a gaping maw. He screamed and tried to pull back but tumbled over onto his side. The other PC froze, horrified, but then started to stomp all the more. It was no good. The semi-conscious punks and skinheads slid aside as the person at the bottom rose, as though a beast from the depths, and with vicious teeth took a bite from the copper's calf. He howled and tried to pull his leg free but the beast was upon him. He pleaded: 'Oh Christ no… no.'

But the wolf cares not what damage it wreaks. The wolf is not for turning. Claws ran down the pig's face, an eyeball slid from its socket. With his good eye he saw the fearsome face of rage, the other hanging down his cheek watched his stomach open as it was torn asunder and his guts slid out, like jelly from an envelope. Much as he tried to pull away, his foot slipped in the blood he'd spilled and in his own that was pouring forth. One of the punks tried to get to his feet and flee but received a rip to his throat. His tumbling body trapped the others on the floor of the van. The inside of the van was a whirlwind of tearing and terror. Blood, flesh and innards painted the inside a modern art disasterpiece.

As another plod reached the van, rocking with the violent tumult inside, a steeled shadow sprang. Its rage was in full flow and was expressed in a sudden sonnet of slashes. Their metre was keen. Left and right bodies dropped and rolled howling on the floor as the beast ran along the street and into the welcoming dark of the night.

All over the capital 'Stannerd' newspaper hawkers went full throttle. More savage slayings in London. WPC Bittner noted that these latest also involved skinheads. Joe knew something wasn't right. He'd been in that van; beyond that he didn't remember a thing. Had a blow to his head knocked him out? If so, how had he got away? Something was weird. There was no way he was going to come forward, that would just be asking for trouble. But he had woken up at home, his clothes blooded, stained, and piled on the floor, with no idea how he'd got there. He didn't think he'd had that much to drink; maybe the booze was something he'd have to consider. This had happened a few times now. It was not something he wanted to think about.

An unease was building in Joe – the pieces were beginning to fit together but they didn't yet make a picture he could recognise. Bittner was starting to put the same pieces together, and for her the picture grew clearer with every single bit of the jigsaw. Was this incident related to murders around Stoke Newington these past few months? WPC Bittner, Joe, and London all wanted to know.

CHAPTER 13

The year 1979 had been chequered. Labour had been struck out of government and Mrs Thatcher was now Prime Minister. There was some great music but the music business had learnt how to commercialise punk. There was black and white, 2 Tone was getting the nation dancing, and that some of it was black was angering some of them that were white.

The Specials were gigging that weekend. A big gig it'd be; the kids embracing the thoughtful danceability the band had to offer would be there in their pork-pie hats and white socks. The skinheads who'd cropped their hair in 1978 after getting into punk and buying into its working class myth would be there. There'd also be the reggae-loving skins happy to be taking a step away from a punk gig. Along with them all would be the angry Nazis, keen to ruin whatever they could, a big gig indeed.

Not that she was aware of all the bubbling undercurrents, but WPC Bittner knew all the top skinhead faces in London would be there. She'd put her skinhead theory to her guv'nors and they agreed. The Met would have officers plotted to nick a murderer. Some in plain clothes looking for a burly, sideburned psycho.

Mark Hazell was a young lad who liked sharp clothes, good music, dancing, and other young lads. All of that was easy but it was often made difficult. He was mates with Ingrid and she knew he liked the 2 Tone bands so suggested he come with her to the gig. He was decked out in 501s with a sewn-in half-inch turn-up above his ankle, oxblood Marten shoes, and a claret Fred Perry with the sky blue and white edging to the collar and sleeves. He looked like a hundred other youths there.

He'd grown up in the Midlands, in Stourbridge, and had left as soon as he could. He'd been bullied through school, for being different. All the time he knew he wasn't that different from half the people bullying him. What really got to them was the fear that he was what they were secretly afraid they were. Mark knew it, and was sensitive to it. He had the sight. Since he was a kid he'd instinctively known things about people. It had started when he was seven and was drinking a cup of tea with his mum – his cup had suddenly leapt up and tipped on its side, the tea spilling out onto the tablecloth.

He'd looked to his mum and said: 'Nan's dead.' Sure enough she had died, just as he'd said.

Mark had lined himself up a little job at the accounts department in an office in London, as well as a bedsit, and moved with all he owned in an Adidas bag. He was happy from the moment he sat on the train. London was big enough to offer something for everyone, big enough that you could be an individual, away from the pressures of a small town, big enough you could find people like yourself.

He'd met Ingrid at work. He liked her sass and the fact that she'd got him straight away. They'd been for beers and seen a few bands together: Swell Maps, The Raincoats, Wire... bands that'd leave most of the kids at his school scratching their heads. Ingrid liked many of the same bands as Mark, and had steered him to some good ones too. She was alright, and so was he.

Tonight was the first time he'd meet her bloke. He'd heard plenty about him, most of it good, but he wondered what they'd make of each other.

Joe had been worded up by Ingrid too, that he'd meet a mate of hers, and that mate was gay. In itself he wasn't too bothered about the bloke being gay, but he was worried about how it'd look to other people.

They met at the gig and Joe's first impression was that Mark looked like everyone else. No reason he shouldn't really, but it wasn't what he'd expected. Mark laughed at the tatty, stained England scarf Joe was sporting round his neck. Joe laughed and said he'd tea-leafed it from a rival. He knew he'd be there that night and was wearing it to wind him up. They both chuckled and drained their drinks. Dennis and the boys were hitting the bar too.

The lad was alright Joe thought, not what he'd worried he might be. He was thinking Mark would be some camp turn but he was funny, smart, and likeable. Joe felt a bit bad for presuming; it was a prejudice and he knew it. There're enough bad things in this world that we should celebrate the good, he was thinking. The Specials had bleakness and tension in their songs, but they also had release and joy.

Mark liked Joe too, could see that he was just a lad, trying hard and doing his best. But he could also sense there was a secret to Joe. One that Joe had an inkling of but didn't really know. Mark could sense the violence around him. It wasn't malevolence as such, more that there was an angry child inside him lashing out. It could be very violent and could touch those around him. Poe put it in his story 'The Bells': 'They are neither man nor woman – They are neither brute nor human –'

For a bubble bath Joe had worn Kessler's tatty scarf to the gig. He showed it off to his mates and regaled them with the tale of how he'd snatched it down on the marshes. The lads drifted into the hall whilst Joe and Mark stayed chatting at the bar. Whilst the lads were deep in discussion Joe was suddenly yanked backwards, his drink flying from his hand. Kessler had made his way up behind him and as he tugged at his scarf that was wrapped around Joe's neck he yelled: 'On me bird and tea leafin' me farkin' scarf. I'll 'ave that back, caant. You can 'ave this.' With that he jerked his knee up and caught Joe's cheek as he was falling back and scrabbling to remain upright. The cheek cracked. Kessler flipped the scarf loosely around his own neck and started to mill punches. Being off balance, and surprised, Joe was in no position to ward off Kessler's blows and boots as they pummelled down on him.

Mark was no fighter and was horrified and stunned by the attack. All the same he stepped forward and swung a punch. It missed. Kessler eyed Mark, leant close and snarled, 'You want to make an occurrence of it?' Mark was rooted to the spot and Kessler gave him a hard shove that sent him staggering back before turning his aggression again toward Joe.

Joe's mates tried to get to him through the crowd, but people were rushing away from the fight and they got stuck in the crush. Again and again Kessler's boot came down on Joe. He was on hands and knees with blood pouring from his cheek and a deep cut on the bridge of his nose. Blood was splattering Kessler's jungle-green army trousers and white Fred Perry shirt. The blood running down Joe's face looked like a macabre willow pattern design on a china plate. Even in Joe's blurring vision he could see the contrast of the red against the white, that was until everything went black and he passed out cold.

CHAPTER 14

When Joe woke up the first thing he saw was gold. Not a golden future but the foil wrapping of a Lucozade bottle standing on top of the small cupboard next to his hospital bed. He ached all over, and not in the way Mills & Boon novelists wrote about. His vision was blurred. He lifted his hands and gently felt his face. He winced as his fingers touched cuts and he could feel the puffiness of swelling.

He looked round the ward. Ingrid was sat on a chair on the other side of the bed. She leant over and Joe asked, 'Do I look pretty?'

'Pretty ugly,' she laughed back.

The light was bright, the whiteness of the hospital walls made it even more so. His eyes were blackened and swollen and the brightness didn't make it any easier to see. He knew he'd taken quite the beating but not what had followed since...

As Kessler was pummelling Joe, Bittner's coppers moved in. The plod were alert as ever and the fight was well under way before they even knew about it. By the time they pushed their way through the crowd watching the fight, Joe was unconscious and Kessler was putting the boot to Joe's ribcage. Two of the plain-clothes officers gave each other the nod – this was their man, they thought – and leapt onto Kessler. They grabbed an arm each and pulled him back. Still raging, Kessler struggled forward, at the same time trying to free himself and get some more kicks in on Joe. The copper gamely hanging on to the left arm gave Kessler a kick to the back of his knee, kept his foot there and pressured down onto his calf muscle. The leg buckled and Kessler was down. More coppers were working their way through the press of people and were piling on. One of them started to read Kessler his rights, or at least shout them in the chaos. At least the arrest would be legal and the crowd of kids now knew they were the Met.

Bittner, face flushed and excited, wormed through the stunned crowd. 'Is it him? Is it him?' she shouted. Looking at Kessler she was quick to make up her mind. He was a big skinhead, bigger than the poor sod he'd just battered. Big and furious, his face contorted with rage. It didn't make him look any less the monster the coppers thought he was. He was spattered with Joe's blood; his football scarf lay on the ground. That had fresh blood on it as well as stains from fights Kessler had been in. He liked to see them as trophies. Bittner scooped it up. Those stains could be evidence.

Kessler fought all the way to the waiting police van, and then inside the van all the way to West End Central nick. As for Joe, he was stretchered out. Bittner was keen to interview him but he was in no state to talk.

Joe was in hospital for several days. He'd taken a few kickings before but nothing as severe as this. Ingrid visited every day, and with the bruises turning yellow from purple and the swelling coming down, Joe was getting back to being himself.

'Pretty ugly,' she laughed back.

She slid her hand under the covers and stroked the cord of his pyjama trousers. 'This seems a bit limp, was it damaged?' she queried.

Joe's rising stiffness seemed to answer not. She moved her hand down and took gentle hold.

Joe gave an 'Ouch'. He rolled slightly to his side. 'I'm throbbing, but not in a good way. Me 'nads are still sore.'

Ingrid laughed and pulled her hand away. 'You'll be home soon, and match fit.' She planted a kiss on his forehead.

Mark Hazell had asked to meet Joe in a quiet caff. Not one where his mates usually ate, but a bit off the manor down the other side of Stamford Hill where it ran down to Tottenham.

After they'd done their initial hellos and chat, Mark cut to the chase: 'You know something's not right, don't you?'

The fact was Joe did, but he wasn't quite sure what Mark was getting at nor if he wanted to say anything.

Mark looked pointedly at the day's *Daily Mirror*, which was lying face up on the caff table, Kessler's picture just under the screaming headline 'CAGED BEAST'. Kessler had been found guilty of the string of murders that had ripped through the city. The picture of him snarling at the judge and jury as he was sent down, all cropped hair, bared teeth, and eyes throwing daggers certainly added to the horror.

It was his scarf that had really tipped the scales of Justice. Sure enough he was vicious and revelled in violence but it was the bloodstains on the scarf that pointed to murder. There were several blood types spattered onto it, many of which matched the blood types of the various victims. The jury had added all of that up and come to guilty. Bittner's hard work had put someone behind bars, the wrong person. Things went no better for her. By the time the case had got to court a superior had made sure he got the credit. Whilst Bittner did get a commendation, it was he who got the promotion and the glory. He made it a point to tell her how good she looked in uniform.

Mark tapped the newspaper. 'I'm glad that tosser is banged up, but those killings weren't him.'

Joe nodded; he knew there was something in himself, he didn't know what.

Mark leant closer across the table, 'The Bible says, "There are spirits that are created for vengeance, and in their fury they lay on grievous torments."'

'I'm Jewish,' replied Joe, somewhat surprised.

'I know,' said Mark, 'it's from Ecclesiasticus. He's one of yours.'

Joe dipped his head and stared at the contorted reflection of his face in the back of a spoon. 'I know there's something going on with me, but I'm not evil.'

Mark paused with his answer as the waitress, an Irish woman in her forties wearing a PG Tips chimps pinny, brought over their food – liver, mash and onions for Mark and a plate of egg and chips in front of Joe.

Mark continued once she'd returned to the counter. 'No, but life's mystery is hidden by the density of flesh.'

Joe's eyes nearly crossed at these deep words from Mark, but he knew the lad was trying to be helpful.

'Joe, one's body is linked to the antagonistic forces that constitute one's soul, and they can be complex and even warring. It's not too far that a spiritual force should take diverse forms.'

Joe wasn't used to this kind of depth in conversation but saw what was being said. It was even weirder that they were being told to him by a lad in a Siouxsie and the Banshees t-shirt and a donkey jacket. Mark lifted a chip from Joe's plate and burst the round yolk of his egg.

'Something is in you,' Mark continued. 'It's not the you that we see every day. It's a raging, angry child. You still have time to do something about it. But don't leave it much longer. You'll hurt the people you love, and much as there is desolation in you, there's love too.'

The words sank home and Joe didn't really hear the rest of the conversation.

Joe was lost in thought nearly all the way home. He knew he'd done some awful things, but the fact was he didn't feel bad about it. There was a monster sat in Downing Street intent on tearing the country apart and eating its beating heart. What was a butchered executive here or there? But like Mark pointed out, how soon before this primal viciousness was loosed upon someone he loved? He should do something, he wasn't sure what. Mark seemed to have an answer but Joe had to want the answer. What to do?

As he turned from the main road towards Ingrid's he heard a familiar beat coming from an open window. He needed to talk through everything running through his head with her. The music got louder as he grew nearer –

'I want all you skinheads to get up on your feet. Put your braces together and your boots on your feet and give me some of that oooooold moonstomping...'

Bestsellers in this Library

Horror
Dr Martenstein – Tim Wells
Wolfamstowe – Tim Wells
The Satanic Rites of Upton Park – Tim Wells
Beast End – Victoria Park
Dr Terror's House of Hot Pants – Victoria Park
Cavorts of the Cover Girl Coven – Victoria Park
The Wanton Witch – Sophie Cameron
The Sound of Violence – Simon Garpunkel
Dracula La Means I Love You – Herbert James
To the Devil a Suedehead – Peyvand Sadeghian
The Hound of the Suburbs – Nicky Tesco
Carrie Go Bring Home – Stephanie King

War
The Stalingraduate – Svetlana Hassel
T-34, Where Are You? – Bill Juniper
The Full Monte Cassino – Bill Juniper
Behind the Rear – Barry Gudden

Thanks to: Peyvand Sadeghian, Cathi Unsworth, John Mitchinson, The Ruts, Phill Jupitus, Mrs Elswood, Lene Lovich, Guen Murroni, Steel Pulse, Chris Low, Booger Bee, Rhoda Dakar, Clare Pollard, Pete Brown, Sophie Cameron, Tapper Zukie, John King, friends and family, Johnny Alucard, Richard Allen, New English Library, and all the *Pan Book of Horror Stories*.

Unbound is the world's first crowdfunding publisher, established in 2011.

We believe that wonderful things can happen when you clear a path for people who share a passion. That's why we've built a platform that brings together readers and authors to crowdfund books they believe in – and give fresh ideas that don't fit the traditional mould the chance they deserve.

This book is in your hands because readers made it possible. Everyone who pledged their support is listed at the front of the book and below. Join them by visiting unbound.com and supporting a book today.

Glenn Airey
Sefer Ana
Imogen Avsec
Gina Baber
Eric Barnes
Graham Barnfield
Jesse Bartels
Andie Berryman
Julia Bird
Sophia Blackwell
Michael Bolger
Thomas Botos
Annie Brechin
Andrew Brown

Joyce Brunelli
Gary Budden
Drew Burke
Garry Bushell
Monty Cantsin
Julie Cheung-Inhin
Andy Ching
Vera Chok
Daniel Cockrill
Stella Coyle
Crittercat
Sarah Cronin
Tom Cullen
Jenny Cumming

Ralph Dartford
Rich Davenport
Katie Della-Valle
Katy Derbyshire
Johnny Dilks
Tony Drayton
Travis Elborough
Daniel Enriquez
Clare Ferguson-Walker
Sam Fisher
Flavio Frezza
Harry Gallon
Draga Geneva
C Geoffrey Taylor
Christian Goetze
Susie Gordon
Niven Govinden
Michael Gratzke
Kathryn Gray
Eamonn Griffin
Deejay Hagler
Steve Harrington
Ella Harrison
Emily Harrison
A.F. Harrold
Bill Herbert
Paul Hodgson
Ulrik Hogrebe
Justin Hopper
Geraint Hughes
Stephen Hutchison
Ainokaisa Huusko
Alice Huzar
Cian Hynes
Mark Hynds
Kirsten Irving
Tali Janner-Klausner
Natalie Katsou
Angela Kirby
Polly Love
Kate Manning
Tom McColl
Yvonne C McCombie

Liam McGurk
Lisa Mckenzie
Ben Moore
Gordon Munro
Guen Murroni
Carlo Navato
Barbara O'Donnell
Niall O'Sullivan
John Osborne
Nii Ayikwei Parkes
Danny Passarella
Ingrid Pitt
Ania Placzkiewicz
James Pogo LoRubbio
Clare Pollard
Gareth Postans
Cina Qedesh
Peter Raynard
Rooby Rooby
Pascal 'Bonbel' Rousse
Liberty Rowley
David Rumsey
Josh Saco
Giuseppe Salvati
Sanghasiha Sanghasiha
Catalina Sapiains Lagos
Mike Schulman
Deborah Scordo Mackie
Jon Seagrave
Jaimie Shorten
Stephanie Smith
Vic Templar
Dean Thatcher
Frank Theis
Chris Toland
Claire Trévien
Rebecca Varley-Winter
Liz Vater
Kim West
Steve White
Tony White
Jennifer Wong
Maor Yavetz